Escape to Freedom

By Ronda Anne Pohner

For Charlie Brown, you are the greatest and for Angela, who encourages me to keep writing.

The Price of Innocence

Kaylee gathered her things and prepared to go home. She dreaded going home. It was the last thing she wanted to do. She often dreamt of disappearing and never returning again, but she knew she couldn't and she wouldn't leave little Joey all alone with him. Kaylee glimpsed at the clock and noted she needed to hustle. It was already 4:30 and she had exactly 30 minutes to pick up Joey and be in the house by 5 PM sharp. The thought of her not making it on time made her cringe. Gregg was so mean. He would make her feel guilty, making her believe she was a bad mother and wife. Kaylee shut down her computer, gathered her things, and headed for her car in the parking lot. She noted many different couples about. They seemed so happy and content. The love they shared was something Kaylee never knew or even dreamed of experiencing with Gregg as his wife. She was trapped in a loveless marriage to a man who barely knew she existed, as long as it suited him.

      Stopping by the daycare center, Kaylee picked up little Joey. He was eleven and asked to attend summer camp rather than stay at home with Gregg, his stepfather. "Mom," stated Joey with great concern, "its 4:47. I don't think we are going to make it." Kaylee's heart sank hearing her child make such a statement. She knew it was not good having Joey around Gregg. She was afraid of this moment when he would be old enough to figure out something was not right in their household. "Yea, we are baby, don't worry about it, everything will be fine." With luck on her side, Kaylee met all green lights and arrived precisely at 4:59. In the living room, sitting in his lounge chair with the remote control, without glancing up or greeting her, he made a deliberate motion while looking at his wristband. He lowered his arm and continued pushing the remote, surfing the cable channels. Joey blindly stated, Good evening, father," and then ran upstairs to wash up. He hated

calling Gregg father. Gregg will never be a good father like
his daddy. Kaylee approached Gregg and sheepishly stated,
"Good evening, Gregg. What would you like to eat for
dinner?" Without looking at her or returning the greeting he
merely stated, "Tuna fish casserole." "Yes, Gregg," replied
Kaylee.

Kaylee placed her things neatly inside the hall
closet as Gregg trained her to do. She immediately went to
the kitchen and washed her hands. Dinner had to be on the
table by 5:30. She quickly gathered all the ingredients
needed and began opening the cans of tuna fish. Joey came
down the stairs and crept to the kitchen. He saw his mother
looked panicked. He smiled warmly at her and without
asking he took out a large pot, filled it with water, and
turned up the burner on the stove under the pot. He went to
the freezer and took out a large Ziploc bag of frozen
cooked elbow macaroni. Kaylee learned to cut time by
having certain foods prepared already and frozen. Kaylee

smiled back and grabbed her little boy as he placed the

frozen pasta on the counter. She gave him a big hug and

whispered I love you in his ear. He squeezed her back.

Together, they prepared the tuna casserole, side salad, soup,

and ice tea. For dessert, Gregg will enjoy vanilla bean ice

cream, Blue Bell, of course. If Kaylee did a good job with

dinner, he would give her and Joey permission to have

dessert as well. If not, they would have to sit at the table

and watch him enjoy the treat. Joey set the table perfectly.

Kaylee placed the food on the table and approached Gregg

in his haven. "Gregg, honey, dinner is served." Gregg

glanced at his wristband and stated, "About time, woman.

You sure are cuttin' it close these days. It's 5:28. You

know I like to stick with my schedule. Don't make me wait

this long again." With her head hung low, she replied,

"Yes, Gregg." After Gregg finished his meal, he gave

Kaylee and Joey permission to have dessert.

   After dinner, Gregg gathered his car keys and went

for a ride. He never stated where he was going and quite

frankly, no one cared. The fact he left the house was always

a treat. Kaylee suspected he was having an affair with

someone else. He probably was Mr. Nice Guy and treating

this girl like she was a queen. He behaved that way with

Kaylee and then everything abruptly changed after they got

married. On their wedding night, he made her stand naked

in front of him, he looked her up and down, and then told

her to redress. He rolled over on the bed, turned off the

lights, and went to sleep. Kaylee was baffled by this

behavior. She did not protest after he screamed at her

earlier for not placing her things neatly in the hall closet.

He grabbed the back of her neck and dragged her to the

closet pushing her face into her handbag and shoes. He

yelled at her some more during dinner when she had not yet

begun to cook it at 5 PM. Kaylee assumed that since it was

their wedding day, he would take her out to eat. Joey was

staying at his cousin's house and had not witnessed such

verbal abuse yet. Kaylee became angry and stated she was leaving him, but quickly rescinded when he grabbed her by the hair and smashed her face against the refrigerator. He told her he would never hurt little Joey as long as she did what he wanted. He flung her to the floor and kicked her in the stomach before releasing the ripped out hair from his grip allowing it to fall atop her.

Gregg leaving gave Kaylee and Joey an opportunity to relax after cleaning the kitchen and other rooms in the house. As a treat, Kaylee made popcorn and got one of their favorite DVDs to watch. Joey was ready for bed just in case Gregg came back early, although he never did on Tuesdays. Gregg was predictable, if not methodical. Every Tuesday was his day to paint the town red with that special someone. He usually came home around 5 or 6 AM expecting Kaylee to get up and serve him breakfast. He always reeked of smoke, cheap perfume, and other unmentionable aromas. Kaylee made it a point to

unofficially declare Tuesday movie night. They gathered
their pillows and blankets and snuggled up in the big sofa
chair. A large bowl of popcorn sat between them on top.
They snuggly secured soda pop between them. During the
movie, Joey matter-of-factly stated, "Mom, he scares me."
Kaylee's heart was filled with despair, for she knew he was
talking about Gregg. She tried to smooth things over and
stated, "Oh, he's not so bad. There are a lot worse people
out there than him. We are very lucky to have such a good
life." Joey sat up straight and nearly knocked over the bowl
of popcorn. "Mom," he almost pleaded, "he's bad. He
treats you so bad. Why does he yell all the time at every
little thing?" Kaylee was speechless, for she knew her son
spoke the truth. "Sweetie, he's just stressed, that's all."
Joey interrupted her and said, "I'm not a baby anymore. I
know what's going on and I know you don't get those
bruises from falling down or bumping into things. What
does he have to be stressed about? He hangs around the

house all day and does nothing while you work hard."
Kaylee began to cry while she placed the soda bottles on
the table.

"Mom, we had a visitor in camp last week that
taught us about domestic violence. I recognize the signs.
Mom, I spoke to him about it." Kaylee was mortified and
wanted to know what he told this person. Joey explained
what he learned about the different types of abuse. With the
utmost sincerity, Joey flatly stated, "Mom, we must leave
this place. We need to go away from here, before he hurts
you really bad." For an eleven-year old, he had great
insight. Kaylee knew her little boy was wise beyond his
years. "Baby, we can't just get up and leave." Joey insisted
they can and even stated how she could go back to school,
get a degree, and have a job she enjoys unlike the one she
has now down at Echo Star, a data entry business. "Joey,
how do you know all this?" she asked. Kaylee looked into
her son's eyes and saw concern so deep it haunted her to

the very core of her being. No eleven-year old should have
to carry such a heavy load as this.

She regretted not leaving Gregg when she had the
chance. She had the perfect opportunity Sunday after the
wedding when she picked up Joey from Cousin Seymour's
house. She should have kept going and never looked back.
Kaylee chose to go back to Gregg mostly out of fear of his
wrath, partly due to the illusion that she could change him,
and partly out of obligation to try to be the perfect wife and
mother her family expected her to be. She didn't want to let
them down. She already felt bad that Gregg did not want
any of them to come down for the ceremony. He arranged
to have them married by a Justice of the Peace. Kaylee was
always driven to please others, much at the expense of her
own happiness. She now regrets that decision. Her
obligation was to raise and protect her son in a loving and
safe environment. She thought she could cover her wounds
with make-up, clothing, and excuses to explain away the

injuries; however, Cousin Seymour didn't buy it and

apparently neither did Joey. The look on Cousin Seymour's

face shamed her when she picked up Joey two days after

the ceremony. She found herself making up an excuse that

she slipped on liquid spilled on the kitchen floor and fell

face first into the refrigerator. She claimed she was carrying

a plate of food and couldn't break her fall. Her story was

simply met with a reserved uh-huh from Cousin Seymour.

Kaylee stroked her son's hair and pushed his bangs

aside. She smiled nervously, unsure of what to do next.

Joey's emerald eyes stared back at her so full of

unconditional love and conviction to not let his mother

suffer anymore. She stroked his cheek and a tear rolled

down her own. "Don't cry, Mom, it will be OK," he

reassured her. Suddenly, a car door slammed. It was Gregg!

He was home way too early. In absolute panic, both of

them jumped up and accidentally spilled the popcorn all

over the floor. Terrified, both of them dropped to their

knees and frantically scooped up fistfuls of popcorn

throwing it back into the bowl. The sound of a key slid into

the keyhole. "Oh my God, no, no…" whispered Kaylee and

tears streamed down her face. She could barely see what

she was doing.

Petrified she would be brutalized in front of her young son,

she urged him to go to bed immediately. "Mom, no, let me

help you, please," pleaded Joey. "Please Joey, I'll be

alright. Now go, quickly…QUICKLY," she

unconvincingly stated. She pushed Joey towards the stairs

and glanced back towards the door as it began to open.

"GO," she forced out between clenched teeth as she pointed

towards the stairs. Joey began to turn away, but courage

stayed his stance. And he defiantly said, "No, not this

time." With a look of incredible shock, Kaylee was numb

from disbelief.

    "What's going on?" asked Gregg through restrained

anger. He stood in the doorway with a 12 pack of beer in

one hand and an opened can in another. Kaylee was

shaking uncontrollably and stuttered, "I, I, accidentally

spilled some popcorn. I'm, I'm sorry Gregg. It was my

fault. We…we were just…" Gregg stepped forward and

asked, "Just what you little bitch, hmmm? WHAT THE

HELL DO YOU THINK YOU ARE DOING?!" He

pointed towards the television. The movie Cars was

playing. Gregg threw the opened can of beer against the

wall and hurled the case of beer at the T.V. smashing the

screen to bits. Cans of beer torpedoed around the room

exploding with such ferocity that Kaylee and Joey were

sprayed with the foamy substance. Getting a running start,

Gregg drop kicked Kaylee so hard she jacked knifed

upward and sailed over the sofa chair. The impact made a

sickening thud sound. Enraged, Joey charged at Gregg and

screamed for him to leave his mother alone. Before he

could make contact with Gregg, Joey was swooped up in

one swift motion and hurled like a rag doll onto the sofa.

Gregg's beef was with the bitch and not the pint-sized pest.

Kaylee was in the process of struggling to crawl away towards the phone to call for help. She was in obvious pain, as she held her midsection with one hand and reached forward to aid her in dragging her body forward. Gregg followed her and repeatedly asked, "What do you think you are doing you stupid bitch?" as he kicked her again and again. Kaylee did not stop her quest to call for help. Gregg walked over her body and snatched the phone off the sofa table. In a singing tone, he cruelly song, "What do you need this for? Who ya gonna call Ghost Busters? Not this time bitch." He took the receiver and cracked it against her skull. "Who are you going to call? No one wants to help you," he spat. In a defensive manner, Kaylee raised her hands to try and protect her face. She pleaded pathetically for him to stop and have mercy. He struck her with such force until the phone disintegrated into bits. Gregg tossed the remaining pieces aside and slowly bent down towards Kaylee. He grabbed her by the hair and lifted

her towards his face. With rancid breath bathed in beer, he

whispered, "Don't EVER touch my television set again.

Now you have to work overtime to buy me another T.V.,

this time a state-of-the art 52 inch LCD." He threw her

down and yelled for her to clean up the mess and then go to

their room for punishment. She was to assume the position.

Kaylee knew he was going to brutally rape her and

humiliate her until she did not have the will to live.

Gregg turned around to deal with the little pest, but

he was gone. The door was ajar with two officers stepping

across the threshold. "Step away from the lady, sir," one

officer demanded. Gregg was stunned to see them at first

and then he began to laugh. "Lady, what lady are you

talking about? She's my bitch and I'm about to remind her

of her place," he chuckled as he grabbed his groin and

grinned. The spoken officer drew his weapon, stepped

forward, and made his request again. Looking down the

barrel of a gun, Gregg did as he was told, for now. They handcuffed him and took him into custody. As they escorted him out, paramedics entered the home and attended to Kaylee's injuries. Gregg saw Joey thank one of the officer's and run into to see his mom. Gregg knew it was time to teach that boy some manners and show him the way of men his style. He couldn't wait to make bail and torture them again. He began to laugh madly.

Joey was not allowed to hug his mom. They kept him at bay as the paramedic team attended to her multiple injuries, secured her into the gurney, and prepared her for transportation. Once she was secured and in the ambulance, Joey was allowed to ride in the back with her, but he had to remain strapped into the safety seat. His mom called out to him and he grabbed a hold of her hand. He was not able to hug or embrace her. "Mom, it's going to be alright." Joey told her how he went to the closet and got out her cell phone after Gregg tossed him on the sofa. Gregg was so engulfed in beating his wife he did not notice Joey slip out

with the phone through the opened door. He dialed the

special number Office Pete made him memorize. It was a

direct line to Officer Pete's cell phone. This is a special cell

that rings in dire emergencies only. He was the person

whom Joey spoke with at camp the previous week. Joey

was relieved that Officer Pete stayed true to his promise of

helping Joey when he called.

Kaylee was amazed at her son's courage. She

smiled warmly at him even though it was very painful to

smile. She spent a couple of weeks in the hospital. Gregg

ruptured her spleen and broke two ribs. She suffered a

bruised kidney and had a serious wound on her head. She

was lucky to be alive. Unfortunately, she did lose the baby.

She was seven weeks pregnant. The baby was a product of

a horrific sexual assault by Gregg. That time, she was late

preparing his meal. Her boss made her work overtime and

she suffered dearly for it. She wasn't sad she lost the baby.

What kind of life could she offer her knowing how brutal
the baby's father enjoyed being? Joey stayed with Cousin
Seymour while Kaylee recovered in the hospital and Gregg
was in the county jail. Cousin Seymour knew far too well
the wrath of Gregg. She was his first cousin once removed.
Gregg's mother was her favorite first cousin. She couldn't
understand where this evilness came from. She had Kaylee
and Joey's personal items removed from his home. It
wasn't much, as Kaylee hadn't been married to Gregg for
more than 6 months. Cousin Seymour knew she had to save
them from him. His first wife died of suicide. Cousin
Seymour didn't believe for a minute that Sarah committed
suicide. She was certain Gregg killed her. He beat Sarah to
a pulp all the time. She arranged to have other family
members in another town take in the two until Kaylee was
able to get back on her feet and find work to start a new
life. Kaylee was most grateful and was hopeful of the
prospects for a new life.

Escape to Nowhere

Kaylee and Joey stayed in Wilcox Co. It's about 20

miles from Suffolk Co., where her previous life ended with

the death of her husband, Joseph. Kaylee will never forget

that day. She and Joseph rented a log cabin in the woods.

They were celebrating their tenth anniversary. Some kid

broke into their cabin. He was covered in blood and had a

fistful of Joseph's clothing. Her husband, being so

protective of her, grabbed the boy and demanded to know

why he was pilfering his property. The boy was terrified

and bewildered. He was a little guy, not too much older

than Joey is now. From nowhere, the boy suddenly had a

gun and shot her husband point blank in the stomach.

Terrified, the boy ran off. Kaylee remembers holding her

dying husband in her arms and screaming at the fleeing

youth. She didn't know why this was happening. She

rushed to the phone at the cabin and called 911. She

returned to her husband and he whispered for her to take

care of their young son, Joey, who was only seven years old. He told her he loved her with all his heart and then he expired in her arms. She remembers later that day, they caught the youth, but he put a bullet in his head from the same gun that took her husband's life. Some days later, they found Old Man Green's dead body across the highway in his truck parked at the junk yard. He was a creepy old man who had an unusual fondness for little boys. They determined the boy was involved in that incident, too. That explained the blood that was all over his clothes. She remembers his name was Caleb.

After losing her husband, Kaylee and Joey moved 500 miles away to Bremer's Den where she eventually met Gregg three years after her husband passed. She often thought about the day he asked her to marry him. It was the same day she learned, Caleb, the boy who killed her husband had died in the hospital. His mother discontinued life support. The boy's father also died the same day.

Feeling like she will never seek the answers to the

questions she so desperately wanted to ask the young man,

she felt depressed and utterly alone. For a few months, she

was dating Gregg. He was such a gentleman. He reminded

her of Joseph. Little Joey needed a father figure and she

thought Gregg was the perfect match. That dreadful day,

Gregg asked her to marry him and she agreed. Kaylee

desperately regrets that decision. Fourteen months have

passed since she married Gregg. She got an annulment and

was happy to be free of him forever. Or so she thought.

Joey was now twelve and in the seventh grade. He

made several friends and even met up with a boy from his

past from Suffolk Co. She had mixed reservations about

Joey's friend Sean. He was the younger brother of Sims,

who happened to be the former best friend of Caleb, the

boy who killed her husband. She did not want Joey to know

the real truth about his father's death. He seemed so happy

and well adjusted. Not even Sean or Sims knew who she

was. One day while picking up Joey from a birthday party at Sean's house, she overheard Sims talking to other kids about Caleb. He spoke so reverently of him, as if this little murderer was some saint. She was caught off guard but managed to not show it. Never in her wildest dreams would she think she would meet up with an associated ghost from her past. She made the choice to keep it to herself, so as not to make anyone feel uncomfortable around her or Joey. Whenever anyone asked about Joey's father, she simply stated he was in a fatal accident and offered no further explanation. She changed her name back to her first married name. She did not want to keep Gregg's last name. No one put two and two together. She was much relieved.

Kaylee made friends quickly. She was happy to have friends again. Gregg did not allow her to have any friends back in Bremer's Den. Her whole existence centered on servitude. Serving him and working in order to provide for him. Her best friend Megan was a Godsend.

She met Megan at church shortly after she arrived in

Wilcox. Megan helped her land a job as a receptionist in a

law firm. This allowed Kaylee to work part time with great

benefits and still attend class at the community college. She

was making more money working part time as a

receptionist than she did working as a data entry clerk.

They helped her get an annulment from Gregg and change

her name back. Kaylee kept in contact with Cousin

Seymour. She was forever thankful for her going out of her

way to make sure Kaylee and Joey were safe. She stayed

about six weeks with family members of Cousin Seymour.

They were very kind and helped her to recuperate. When

Kaylee heard Gregg was going to be released from jail

soon, she gathered her things along with Joey and moved

away. Kaylee was awarded $7000 in restitution from Gregg

and she cleared out the bank account, totaling $15,556 in

all. She took that money in cash and started a new life. It

was her money anyway. She also sold her car. Some of it

was left over from the insurance policy on Joseph. Most of

that money went to pay off their debts.

Life was good. Kaylee and Joey were happy and

content. After landing the receptionist job, she rented a two

bedroom home. It was beautiful. She threw her handbag

and shoes anywhere she pleased. Her cabinets were not

arranged in any particular order. Magazines and old

newspapers were strewn over the coffee table. No body

cared. Her house was not dirty or filthy. She just did not

care if things were not in an exact order or sequence as

Gregg required. She purposely left her bed unmade. They

ate whenever they felt like it. Life was great.

It was a Friday afternoon, around 2 pm. Joey was

still in school until 3:30, and then he had soccer practice

after school. She planned to pick him up around 5:30 for

their dinner date at the local pizza joint. Kaylee did not

have class that afternoon. She never did on Fridays. She

looked forward to going home to relax for a few hours

before picking Joey up. She pulled up into her driveway

and parked her 2008 Dodge Caravan. It was such a nice

vehicle. Kaylee and Joey took the van camping near

Dillon's Hole once a month. The van was roomy enough

for them to sleep indoors; however, they preferred to set up

camp and pitch a tent instead. Sleeping under the stars was

one of her favorite pastimes for Kaylee. It reminded her of

the special times she had with Joseph. She always felt his

presence whenever she and Joey went camping. They never

slept in the tent, but they did sleep in the van a couple times

after the sky opened up and brought forth the rains. Joey

liked that the van had two DVD players and he could watch

a movie on one while playing a video game on another.

Several times, Megan and her son Zach joined them. Zach

was two years younger than Joey, but they still had fun

together. During one of those campouts, Kaylee shared her

horrific experiences with Megan, a divorced mother who

also was a victim of domestic violence; however, nowhere

near the horror that Kaylee endured. She understood the

importance of keeping this matter between the two of them.

They seemed to draw comfort and counsel from one

another.

Kaylee parked the van under the carport in the

driveway. She waited a moment before exiting the vehicle.

Roberta Flack's *Killing Me Softly* played on the radio. That

was her favorite song that Joseph sang to her while playing

his guitar. Thinking about the guitar saddened her. She

brought it with her to Bremer's Den, but soon after the

wedding, Gregg smashed it to bits and did not allow her to

keep anything that reminded her of Joseph, especially

photographs. She managed to secure one in a safe place, the

bible, before he could rip it up like he did the others.

Kaylee didn't think she could feel any lower than how she

felt that day. Joseph's guitar was beyond repair. Gregg

made her throw it in the trash out back, but not before he

took the strings and whipped her until she bled. Out of

desperation, she kept one of strings by winding it up into a tight circle and sliding it inside her sleeve. She double rolled her sleeves to ensure it did not fall out before she could find a suitable hiding place.

When she entered the door, Gregg grabbed her by the nape of the neck and forced her to the floor. The rolled up string fell from her sleeve and in the commotion, without noticing Gregg accidentally kicked it under the sofa out of sight. She was made to pick up all the ripped photographs and then tear them into tiny bits with her own hands. The floor was soaked with her tears. Gregg made her scoop up all the pieces in her hand and if she left one piece on the floor, he smacked her so hard until she spilled the remaining pieces. This game continued until she managed by sheer will to not spill any pieces. Her hands were so gently cupped around the torn images of her beloved Joseph though they shook from terror. Gregg became tired of the game and with one hand he slapped her cupped hands upwards and the pieces hit the ceiling before flying everywhere. He laughed and told her to have it cleaned up by the time her returned from playing poker with his buddies. Kaylee remembers spending the whole night finding all the pieces that were so cruelly strewn about the living room. After she moved into her new home, she took the protected photo of Joseph in the bible and made copies of many sizes. She placed a large 11 x 14 framed photo in Joey's room. It seemed to make him feel more at ease knowing his father watched over him. She had an 8 x 10 frame custom made to hold her beloved Joseph on the mantel of the fireplace. She kissed him every morning when she left for work and every evening when she returned home. She had pictures of Joseph at work and in her wallet. He was never far from her.

Kaylee closed the van door and picked up the evening newspaper. Her wallet accidentally fell out of her handbag. She picked it up and did not return it to the bag.

She checked the mailbox for mail and then went into the

house with the thrill of drawing a warm bath. She loved her

Friday afternoon-before-I-pick-up-Joey baths. It relaxed her

so. She enjoyed buying different fragrances for her bath

water. She always lit candles and put on soft classical

music. It was her favorite day of the week. Kaylee walked

into the door, dropped her car keys and wallet on the table

in the entry, and noted a different aroma. It was a pungent

smell and seemed somewhat familiar. She was perplexed

but pushed the thought aside in anticipation of her bath.

She went to the mantel to continue her ritual and was

stunned to see the picture of Joseph was lying face down.

She figured she must not have placed it back properly that

morning and it fell over when she exited the house. She

picked it up, kissed it, stroked the glass, and then placed the

frame back in its proper position.

Anxious to draw her bath, Kaylee threw the daily

newspaper on the coffee table as she ran upstairs, tossing

her handbag onto the sofa, and kicking her shoes off along

the way. She did not notice the magazines and newspapers

were neatly placed like a fan on the coffee table in

alphabetical and chronological order. Like a child, Kaylee

took the stairs two at a time. She went directly to the master

bathroom and drew water in the tub. Placing two fingers

under the running water, she waited until the temperature

was just right before she stopped adjusting the knob. She

placed the plug in its place and then thought for a moment

about which bubble bath she wanted to pour into the water.

She decided on strawberries and crème. As she poured a

capful into the water, she felt a little playful and decided

she wanted an extra bubbly bath, so she put another capful

in. The aroma immediately rose to meet her nostrils and she

drew in a deep breath. Humming, she disrobed and went to

her walk-in closet located in the bathroom. She opened the

door and began her selection for a robe. She had several to

choose from. Being in such a state of euphoria, Kaylee did

not notice the pungent odor masked by strawberries in

crème that hung heavily in the closet's air. She selected her

favorite fluffy white robe, closed the closet door, and

carried it to the master suite. She was not concerned about

anyone seeing her in the buff, so she did not bother to close

the bedroom door. Kaylee selected a warm-up suit from the

dresser drawer and placed her clothes on the bed. She went

directly to her Sony six CD changer sound system and put

on a favorite CD, Don Juan by Richard Strauss, followed

by several other composers to take their rightful turns. The

chord progression was so invigorating; she flitted about the

room pretending to dance with Joseph in her arms. She

swung around and around and almost forgot about the bath

water. She went to the tub and turned off the water. The air

was thick with moisture sporting a slight strawberry

fragrance and the bathroom mirrors were fogged up. Still in

a playful mood, she wrote "I love you, dear Joseph" on the

misty surface. Then she leaned forward and kissed the

mirror, leaving her lip print. She took a lighter out of the drawer to light the candles.

Kaylee turned to her bath and was about to step into it when she noticed the closet door was ajar. Thinking she must have forgotten to close it, she did so and then returned to her bath. She lit three candles standing on the rim of the tub then she stepped into the tub and slid down slowly, allowing her skin to adjust to the temperature. Kaylee was absolutely thrilled to soak in her hot bath filled with strawberries and crème aromas. Instrumental music played on the CD in the other room and all was good. Tons of fragrant bubbles danced about her person. She could feel her muscles relaxing and surrendering to such pleasurable therapy. Kaylee closed her eyes and enjoyed the moment.

After the first CD played in its entirety, Kaylee opened her eyes and began to sponge herself. She slipped down into the tub to wet her hair before shampooing it with matching strawberries and crème conditioning shampoo. It was a ritual for her to always match the bubble bath, body

wash, and shampoo. It made her universe whole. She

washed her hair, applied matching conditioning lotion, and

leaned back into the tub before rinsing it out. It was part of

her ritual to allow the foamy substance to soak into her hair

and condition it thoroughly. After about ten minutes, she

slid down into the tub and stayed there as long as she could.

She opened her eyes and thought she saw a passing

shadow. Immediately, Kaylee sat up and water gushed

down her face. A tidal of water waved over the candles and

extinguished the flickering flames. She wiped her eyes with

her bathing sponge and looked around. The closet door was

ajar. Kaylee knew she closed that door.

Fearful that someone may have broken into her

home, she decided it was time to get out of the tub. As she

stepped out of the tub, she noticed the mirror had a residual

effect on it. The name Joseph was crossed out. Kaylee was

petrified. Without drying off, she put on her robe and went

into the bedroom. She looked around nervously and decided to close the door. She locked it. Terrified that someone was in the room with her while she was in such a vulnerable state; she quickly dressed while keeping watch over the bathroom. It was difficult to get her clothes on, as they stuck to her wet skin. Nervously, she went back into the bathroom to retrieve running shoes from the closet. She slowly walked to the closet, but not before picking up the plunger near the toilet. She figured she could use the handle as a weapon. After inspecting the closet, she grabbed her shoes and put them on quickly. She also made a mental note that the closet smelled differently, more like it did that morning before she left for work, and less like it did as she drew her bath.

With extremely wet hair and matted clothing, Kaylee cautiously took the stairs one step at a time. She still had the plunger with her, intending to use it. She went to grab her handbag off the sofa and noticed the arrangement of magazines and newspapers. Even the paper

she threw on the table before her bath was neatly placed.

She looked onto the sofa, but her handbag was not there.

She chose to not kiss the picture of Joseph before exiting

the room. She did, however, notice his picture was face

down. Scared beyond belief, she ran out of the house

without retrieving her handbag for she had a hunch it was

in the closet, along with the shoes she discarded and were

no longer strewn about on the floor where she left them.

Kaylee grabbed her wallet and keys but did not bother to

lock the door as she frantically exited. With the key remote

she unlocked the car door and first quickly searched the

inside of car with her eyes before getting in it and driving

away. She still had another hour before she needed to pick

up Joey. She went directly to Megan's house. Kaylee had a

bad feeling.

Teasing the Prey

Frightened at the prospects of having Gregg invade

her life, Kaylee nervously checked her rearview mirror for

signs that she was being followed. She managed to call

Megan on the phone. Lucky for her, Megan was not home.

She was at the soccer practice watching Zach practice

blocking the goals. Joey and Zach were on a local boys' 10-

12 team. Kaylee did a U-turn and headed towards the field.

She arrived around 4:55 PM. Joey had the ball and passed it

to another player. Megan met Kaylee at her van and sat in

the front seat. Megan noted how distraught she looked with

her hair partly wet and uncombed. Kaylee explained what

transpired. Megan was mortified and asked Kaylee if she

wasn't imagining things. Kaylee described in detail the

events again. She shook violently and raised her hands to

her cheeks. "Megan, what am I going to do?" The thought

of Gregg breaking into her home and playing mind games

on her unnerved her, but not as much as the thought that

she stood naked in front of him without noticing. This made her feel extremely dirty and filthy even though she just took a bath. She felt so unclean and violated. She was thankful he did not overpower her and force himself upon her.

Megan insisted Kaylee and Joey come home with her. Kaylee protested and did not want to put her and Zach at risk, but Megan would hear none of it. "What do I tell Joey?" asked Kaylee. Megan reached over, took her friend's hand, and softly stated, "The truth. Tell him the truth. We will explain to the boys that it is too dangerous for you to go home. Right now, we call the police." Joey glanced over and saw his mom's van. A big smile came across his face, but quickly disappeared when he saw his mom appeared to be in distress. Instinct told him something was very wrong. Nevertheless, he finished his practice without distraction, but kept an eye on the visual interaction between the two ladies sitting in the van. He saw Megan call someone on her cell phone.

Megan dialed a friend at the local police station. She was someone who helped her out when she was having problems with her then abusive husband. Officer Riley agreed to meet them at Kaylee's house around 6 PM. After soccer practice was finished, Joey ran to his mom's van and opened the driver's side door. Zach was close by his side and stood behind Joey. "Hi, Ms. Baker," greeted Joey, as he looked past Kaylee and smiled warmly at Megan. He then turned his attention to his mom after Megan greeted him back and her son Zach. "Mom, what's wrong? What happened?" Joey reached out with his dirty hands and put his right hand on her shoulder and left hand on her arm. "Nothing, baby, I just, I don't know," she hesitated. Joey looked her and gently grabbed a fistful of her hair. "Mom, you look terrible. You would never leave the house with your hair lookin' whacked out." Kaylee couldn't help but laugh nervously. Her son stared at her quizzically. Kaylee looked to Megan for guidance.

Megan briefly explained the situation to the boys and they agreed to settle for take out pizza and eat it at Megan's house. The ladies were not concerned about the boys' safety, for they would busy themselves with video games all night. Kaylee was too distraught to explain all of this and she was grateful to have such a special friend like Megan.

They arrived a little after 6 at Kaylee's house. Officer Riley's cruiser was parked out on the street. As Kaylee pulled into the driveway, Officer Riley exited the cruiser and crossed the yard to speak with the ladies. "Good evening, ladies," stated Officer Riley. "I understand there may have been a break in at this residence?" Kaylee was apprehensive, but Megan encouraged her to tell her story. She explained what had happened. After she finished, Officer Riley explained how she did an initial check on the outside perimeter of the home and only found the front door unsecured. She stated she did not enter the home. She

asked permission to inspect the home alone. Kaylee agreed

and Officer Riley went in alone.

    After 10 minutes she exited the home and stated it

was empty. Together, all three entered the home so that

Kaylee can walk Officer Riley through her afternoon.

Kaylee walked into the door and heard classical music

playing. She did not notice any unusual smells. She figured

the opened front door aired out the home. The first thing

she noticed was Joseph's picture was upright and in it's

proper place. The newspapers and magazines looked as if

they were dropped from mid-air onto the coffee table. Her

handbag was thrown on the sofa and her shoes were strewn

on the floor, but not quite in the same place. Kaylee

couldn't explain these things. She felt as if she were going

crazy. Kaylee took the two upstairs and was convinced

someone was still hiding in the bathroom closet. Her room

was as she left it. The last CD played on the sound system.

The white fluffy towel was thrown on the floor near the bed. The bathtub was filled with cold water, although the suds were gone. A lighter lay deep in the water along with her bath sponge. The candles were not lit, in fact, the indentation surrounding the wick held puddles of liquid. The closet door was closed. She did not want to open it, so Officer Riley opened it and inspected all the nooks and crannies. Nothing, absolutely nothing she described at the soccer field was evident. Kaylee felt humiliated and embarrassed.

Officer Riley began asking her questions about work and anything else that may have stressed her out. Kaylee could not understand what happened, but she knew what she saw. Megan put her arm around Kaylee and squeezed her shoulders. "I want you to stay with me for a few days," she whispered to her. Officer Riley gave Kaylee her business card, squeezed her arm in reassurance, and asked her to call her if something unusual should come up again. After the officer left, Kaylee broke down crying.

Megan walked her to the bed and comforted her. After she

composed herself, Megan helped her pack some items for

both she and Joey. They cleaned up the bathroom. The

ladies went downstairs and gathered her handbag. Kaylee

picked up the bag and noticed some items were missing.

She knew she had her work access I.D. card in her bag,

along with her favorite tube of lotion. She went to the hall

closet and opened the door. She didn't see these items until

she picked up a bag that fell over. Beneath it was her access

card and lotion. Stunned at this discovery, Megan took out

her cell phone and started to dial Officer Riley to report

their findings, but Kaylee grabbed Megan by the arm and

insisted they leave immediately. Both ladies knew she did

not imagine it.

Kaylee locked up the house and asked Megan to

drive instead. She was too nervous and distraught to

concentrate on the road. Megan was more than happy to

oblige. "Kaylee, both of you are more than welcomed to stay with us for awhile. Look, we are going to figure this out," she promised. Kaylee cried softly to herself. "How do you think he found us? I mean, I never told him I lived over here. When I met him, I just wanted to forget my past and move on. I just don't understand," replied Kaylee through tears and gasps of air. "Well, do you think Cousin Seymour said anything to Gregg?" Kaylee was adamant that she would not have given up her location like that. Megan insisted she call Cousin Seymour first thing in the morning to see what was going on. Kaylee and Joey got settled in. Zach had bunk beds so it made it easy to find a place for Joey to sleep. Zach was afraid of heights, so Joey took the top bunk. After the boys were settled in for the night, Kaylee and Megan chitchatted in the kitchen over a cup of coffee and day old pastries. Both of them agreed to always carry the essentials of their wallet and keys at all times, in case of an emergency. Kaylee felt better and was ready for

bed. Megan had a three-bedroom home. The third bedroom
was an office that had a sofa in it. Kaylee lay down, but she
had a difficult time falling asleep right away. She was eager
to speak to Cousin Seymour. Many thoughts invaded her
mind and kept her on edge. Eventually, she drifted off to
sleep out of pure exhaustion.

Megan stayed up a little longer to clean up the
kitchen. When she was satisfied, she threw the rag in the
sink and turned off the light; just after she turned around to
head to her bedroom, a shadow passed by the kitchen
window. The hair on the back of her neck stood up and
something urged her to turn around. Nothing seemed out of
the ordinary. She told herself she was being silly and went
back to the sink to peer out the window. Everything seemed
fine. She sighed and went to bed, but not before checking
the doors and windows one last time. Megan chuckled at
herself for being so paranoid. "Get a grip, old gal, one of us
needs to remain sane," she told herself.

Outside the boy's bedroom window, a shadowed

figure peered into the window. The curtains were drawn

and the blinds were partly closed. The shadowed figure was

able to catch a glimpse of the boys sleeping in their bunks.

He tried the window, but it was locked. As he turned away,

his foot hit a garden shovel, which made a scraping noise.

The neighbor's dogs responded with a symphony of barks.

The shadowed stranger left the premises. The barking dogs

awoke Kaylee; she looked out her window and saw a man

walking away from the property. He appeared to have the

same build as Gregg, but more slender. Kaylee was deeply

frightened. "What is it?" asked Megan as she stepped

through the door bathed by the hallway light. Kaylee

jumped and screamed. "I'm sorry, it's only me. Are you

OK? What's wrong?" asked Megan. Kaylee explained how

she was awaken by the dog barking and saw a man leave

the yard. "I also heard Jack barking. He never barks unless

someone bothers him." Megan went to the window and

peeked through it. She did not see the man. The street was

dimly lit and offered no clear view in any direction. He was

gone. Megan insisted Kaylee stay with her in her room. She

had a queen-sized bed, which was more than

accommodating. Kaylee felt better having Megan by her

side. Little did they know the mysterious man watched

them from the shadows; he was across the street just two

houses down, grinning like an evil madman.

The next morning, Megan awoke and found Kaylee

was up and about. The smell of freshly brewed coffee

teased her senses. Taking in a deep breath, she swung her

legs over the side of the bed. Sleepiness still held her

hostage. She lingered a bit longer before getting up to

shower. They boys were awake and already watching

cartoons in the living room. As Megan came downstairs,

she greeted the boys and asked Zach if he brushed his teeth

yet. Zach sighed and replied no. Both of the boys got up to

tend to this tedious task. Megan went into the kitchen and

was surprised to see Kaylee had prepared a wonderful

spread. She had hotcakes, egg omelets, and sausage

prepared. The table was already set with orange juice ready

for the boys. "Wow, this is awesome. You are going to

spoil us, Kaylee. We are used to simply Lucky Charms,"

she giggled. Kaylee smiled warmly and invited her to sit

down and enjoy the meal. As Megan sat down she called to

the boys to wash their hands and join them for breakfast. "I

hope you don't mind, Megan. I wanted to show my

appreciation." Megan laughed and stated, "You don't need

my permission to whip up something like this. My house is

your house. I didn't have sausage and pancake mix. Did

you go out?" Kaylee explained how she got up pretty early

and went to the store to acquire the goods. Megan was

worried about Kaylee going off by herself, at least, until

they could figure out what was going on. "I know, Megan,

but I refuse to be a caged animal. Joey and I will stay

through the weekend, but Sunday night, we have to go back

home. I worked too hard to let this monster run me off from

my home."

      After breakfast, Joey and Zach went to play catch

with a couple of brothers from the neighborhood in their

backyard. Although a little worried that Joey was away

from her, Kaylee felt confident he would be OK as long as

he remained with the group. The ladies cleaned up the

kitchen and talked about the shadowy figure last night. "I

think we need to inform Officer Riley what happened last

night. It might be important," stated Megan. Kaylee sighed.

She knew her dear friend was right. She just did not feel it

necessary to drag all of these people into her life. She

blushed at the thought of looking foolish yesterday in front

of Officer Riley. "Huh, she must think I am a nut case,"

stated Kaylee. "Nah, I don't think so. She's a cop, Believe

me, she's come across more serious nut cases than you."

Both ladies laughed. Kaylee felt a little better. Megan

definitely had the humor gene. She could always make her

laugh. "I think you should call that Cousins Seymour. Find out what she knows." Kaylee agreed and picked up the landline phone. It was dead. "That's weird, there is no dial tone," Kaylee reported. Megan was surprised and tried the line herself. She was unable to get a dial tone. "That's strange. I don't understand this. Hmm, you don't think that person did something to the line, do you? Kaylee shrugged. They decided to check out the line and went out back. Megan opened the box and sure enough, the phone was not just disconnected, but the wires were obviously cut with a sharp object. Kaylee stood slowly and looked around nervously. "I think we need to call Officer Riley right now. I will use my cell."

She pulled out her cell phone and dialed Officer Riley's number. She got her voice message machine. Megan left a brief message describing the events surrounding the strange man in their yard last night and the dead phone line. She left both her and Kaylee's numbers for contact purposes. Megan was disappointed that she was unable to reach Officer Riley. In the past, the one person she knew she could count on was Officer Riley. "Well, Megan, it is the weekend. She probably took a few days off," reassured Kaylee. She will get the messages when she returns. I think I'll call Cousin Seymour now. I have lots of questions to ask her.

The Courage to Find Courage

Kaylee and Megan reentered the home and locked the door behind them. With her cell phone, Kaylee dialed Cousin Seymour's number. The phone rang several times before someone picked up the line and hung up immediately. Perplexed, Kaylee redialed. The phone rang half a dozen times before a nervous Cousin Seymour answered the line. "Hello?" asked the shaky voice on the other line. "Cousin Seymour? It's me Kaylee. Is everything alright?" There was no response on the other end. Silence spoke back volumes and it scared Kaylee. "Cousin Seymour? Hello? Cousin Seymour?" asked Kaylee with urgency. "*Kaylee*," whispered the shaky voice, "*run.*" Kaylee's skin crawled and the hair on the back of her neck stood straight and tall. "Cousin Seymour, is that you? What's wrong? Is someone hurting you?" A strange noise was heard in the background. "*Kaylee, you cannot help me, it's too late. Run, Kaylee, **RUN**, they're coming...for you,*" faded the eerie voice. A loud thud was heard and a woman

screamed a death cry. The phone was disconnected and the

call was lost. Megan's eyes were wide as pie pans and

searched Kaylee's face for answers. Kaylee slowly closed

her cell phone and looked off into nothingness. Megan

reached to grab her hand and it was ice cold. Her hands

shook so violently. "What's wrong, what happened?

Kaylee? Who was that?" asked Megan impatiently yet with

great concern.

"Cousin Seymour is in trouble. She needs my help,"

stated Kaylee matter-of-factly. "She says someone is

coming for me. She used the word they. Who are they? I

must go back to Bremer's Den and find out what is going

on." Megan was dumbstruck. "What, are you nuts? You

can't go back there." Kaylee didn't know what came over

here, but she knew deep in her heart, she had to go back

and face her fears. She felt compelled to help Cousin

Seymour. "Kaylee, think about what you are doing. It

sounded like someone was holding Cousin Seymour

hostage. What if she is injured or dead even? What can you

do for her? This is crazy. I won't let you go back alone. No

way, we stick together." Kaylee was deeply moved by

Megan's loyalty, but she did not want to put her friend in

jeopardy. She felt she had already done so.

It was Saturday, late morning. Kaylee began

packing up her things, somewhat ignoring the pleas from

Megan to not undertake this crazy task. Kaylee was

determined to help Cousin Seymour. Although they were

not blood relatives, she felt compelled to help the one

woman who helped her through the most difficult time of

her life. She was a Godsend. Cousin Seymour was only a

call away when Kaylee needed her to pick up Joey and

keep him for a day or two. This was always when Gregg

used her as a punching bag and left reminders of the event

on her body in plain view. She would call in sick to work

out of shame, but she would not stay home. She pretended

to go to work and used her emergency cash to stay at a

hotel in a nearby town during work hours. Kaylee was

never worried about Gregg finding out, because they only

had one working car. Megan gave up and walked out of the

room out of frustration. She tried to call Officer Riley, but

she was off-duty and not available. Megan left a message

about her concerns. By the time Kaylee was finished

packing her things, Megan presented herself with a packed

bag and sternly stated, "We are in this together." Kaylee

was moved by her friend's undying allegiance to her cause.

Megan would not take no for an answer and even made

arrangements for the boys to stay over at a neighbor's

house for a few days. That afternoon, they were going

camping at Dillon's Hole and Kaylee knew Joey was

familiar with the area and would be comfortable. They

were already playing ball together, so Kaylee was OK with

the idea. Kaylee sighed and surrendered.

　　　Together they packed up the boys' things. While

Megan took the bags over to the neighbor's house and

explained things as simply as possible to the boys, Kaylee

went to the kitchen to prepare food for the long journey.

Kaylee knew the trip would take about 8 hours. She packed

a few sandwiches, a box of Cheez-It® Crackers, a few bags

of trail mix, and placed six bottles of water and ice cubes in

a small portable cooler. Satisfied that she packed enough

food, Kaylee placed the loose food items and napkins into a

plastic bag and prepared to carry it along with the ice chest

to the car. She heard the front door open and swung around

to hand Megan the bag so they could carry it to the car.

Gregg stood before her, smirking, singing, "Remember me,

bitch?" He punched her in the face causing Kaylee to drop

the cooler and snack bag. Ice cubes spilled out onto the

floor and the bottles of water rolled in different directions.

Kaylee fell backwards and used her arms to break her fall.

She was shocked and stunned. Her nose was bleeding and

she felt as if front teeth were loosened.

Gregg approached Kaylee, crushing ice under his boots. He picked her up by the hair and dragged her to the kitchen table. He slung her over the table and began to choke her with one hand while he held onto a fistful of hair with another. Kaylee was terrified and tried to prey his grip from her throat. He kept yanking her hair, making her head hurt. She found it difficult to breathe. Not willing to succumb to this tyrant, Kaylee fought back by kicking him as hard as she could and wiggling side to side. Gregg was surprised to see new courage and strength in Kaylee. He was used to a submission wimp to which he could manipulate as he pleased. This aroused him sexually and he wanted to conquer her even more so. Gregg released his grip on her hair and slapped her off the table. She fell onto the chair, which tipped over landing her on her side. Gregg licked his lips and smoothed back his hair with one hand. "Were gonna have a real good time, you and me. I'm gonna show you what they did to me in jail, bitch. You won't be able to sit for a week when I'm done with you," he

promised as he began to undue his belt buckle. The front

door opened and Megan walked in. "Kaylee, are you

ready?" she called out. Kaylee tried to answer back and

warn her to run away, but her throat felt crushed and her

loose teeth made it difficult to annunciate properly. Kaylee

tried to speak but nothing came out. Megan could see the

ice spilled on the floor along with the other items Kaylee

wanted to carry to the car. Instinct told her that something

was wrong. Before she could react, a tall slender man

appeared. He had semi-long hair that needed cutting. It was

stringy, greasy, and in need of serious shampoo and

conditioning. The man's face was somewhat long and his

eyes were set too close together. He had a scar on his left

cheek that appeared to be a recent injury. His clothing was

wrinkled. He had a dirty T-shirt on and black dusty jeans.

He wore black workman's boots. A tattoo with the name

Kaylee and a knife sticking out of a broken heart was

colored on his right arm from the elbow to the wrist. The most striking feature was his gray eyes. They seem to darken as they looked back at Megan. His belt buckle was undone and flapping up and down as he moved slowly towards her. "Hmm, who is this? A pretty little thing you are. I bet you're a better fuck than that stingy whore." He licked his lips and cracked a smile. Megan didn't have to ask who this was. She knew by the look in his eyes and his demeanor.

     "Get the hell out of my house," demanded Megan. Gregg laughed a wicked laugh. Megan stood her ground, something she learned in her past experiences, and refused to show any signs of weakness. Gregg mocked her, mimicking her words as he began to circle around the sofa in anticipation of ripping her clothes off and violating her. Out of nowhere, Kaylee came up swiftly behind him and whacked him as hard as she could on the back of the head with a skillet. The crack was magnificent and Gregg went down without a fight. Immediately, Kaylee ran to Megan.

She limped from the injury she received when Gregg

slammed her on top of the table. Without saying anything,

both ladies went to Gregg to assess his condition. Concern

that he would regain consciousness, Megan produced rope

from the hall closet to bind his arms behind his back. While

there, she slipped pepper spray in her pocket in case he was

uncooperative. Kaylee used her cell phone to call police.

Seconds after she hung up, Officer Riley appeared at the

front door. She was dressed in civilian clothing and asked

what was going on. Megan was happy to see her and stated

how Gregg entered her home illegally and terrorized

Kaylee. "Oh yea?" asked Officer Riley, as she peered

behind her and then closed the door. She went to Gregg and

knelt down, feeling his pulse, as he moaned. She turned

him on his side. Gregg opened his eyes and stared at the

officer.

    "I can take it from here ladies," stated Officer Riley,

as she began to untie Gregg. Megan and Kaylee both told

her to stop and call for backup because he is a dangerous

man. Gregg chuckled and groaned from the pain in the

back of his head. "Officer Riley took our her cell phone and

canceled the call. "Oh, come now, ladies, he's not

dangerous. He's just a puppy dog." She untied him and

helped him to his feet. He was quite wobbly and put his

hand on the back of his head. Blood trickled down his arm.

"Thanks, sis," declared Gregg. "No problem, baby

brother," grinned Officer Riley, "Now, which one of you

ladies assaulted my brother?"

Other books by Ronda Anne Pohner:

A Collection of Short Stories

Gemini

Kristian

Mein Deutsches Book 1

Old Man Johnson's Farm

The Curse of Guadalupe de Inca

The Fallen Child King

The Gaskin Family Clan

The Life of Caleb

The Lighthouse Resident